STAR WARS

THE CLONE WARS™

THE HOLOCRON HEIST

Adapted by Rob Valois

Based on the TV series *STAR WARS: THE CLONE WARS*

Grosset & Dunlap • LucasBooks

GROSSET & DUNLAP
Published by the Penguin Group
Penguin Group (USA) Inc., 375 Hudson Street, New York, New York 10014, USA
Penguin Group (Canada), 90 Eglinton Avenue East, Suite 700,
Toronto, Ontario M4P 2Y3, Canada
(a division of Pearson Penguin Canada Inc.)
Penguin Books Ltd., 80 Strand, London WC2R 0RL, England
Penguin Group Ireland, 25 St. Stephen's Green, Dublin 2, Ireland
(a division of Penguin Books Ltd.)
Penguin Group (Australia), 250 Camberwell Road, Camberwell, Victoria 3124,
Australia
(a division of Pearson Australia Group Pty. Ltd.)
Penguin Books India Pvt. Ltd., 11 Community Centre, Panchsheel Park,
New Delhi—110 017, India
Penguin Group (NZ), 67 Apollo Drive, Rosedale, North Shore 0632, New Zealand
(a division of Pearson New Zealand Ltd.)
Penguin Books (South Africa) (Pty.) Ltd., 24 Sturdee Avenue,
Rosebank, Johannesburg 2196, South Africa

Penguin Books Ltd., Registered Offices:
80 Strand, London WC2R 0RL, England

This book is published in partnership with LucasBooks, a division of Lucasfilm Ltd.

The publisher does not have any control over and does not assume any responsibility
for author or third-party websites or their content.

The scanning, uploading, and distribution of this book via the Internet or via any
other means without the permission of the publisher is illegal and punishable by law.
Please purchase only authorized electronic editions and do not participate in or
encourage electronic piracy of copyrighted materials. Your support of the
author's rights is appreciated.

Library of Congress Cataloging-in-Publication Data is available.

ISBN 978-0-448-45246-3   10 9 8 7 6 5 4 3 2 1

GLOSSARY

Here are some *Clone Wars* terms that might help
you along the way.

Bounty Hunters: Ex-soldiers
or criminals who will do
anything for the right price.

Clawdite: Lizard-like
humanoids from the planet
of Zolan. They are one
of the few shape-shifting
species in the galaxy, and are
sometimes referred to as changelings.

Coruscant: The capital of the galaxy and home of the Jedi
Council.

The Force: An energy field created by all living things. It
gives the Jedi their power.

Galactic Republic: The
government that rules the
galaxy.

Holocron: A crystal device
that the Jedi use to store information.

Hologram: A projected image of a person.

Jedi: Masters of the Force. They use their power to protect the Republic.

Jedi Council: The group of twelve Jedi Masters who oversee all the Jedi in the galaxy.

Jedi Temple: The headquarters of the Jedi. It is located on the planet Coruscant.

Lightsaber: The weapon of a Jedi. It looks like a sword made of colored energy.

Padawan: A young Jedi in training.

Separatist Alliance: The group trying to take over the Galactic Republic.

Sith Lords: Masters of the dark side of the Force and the enemy of the Jedi.

CHAPTER 1

Anakin Skywalker's Padawan, Ahsoka Tano, had been assigned the duty of guarding the Archives in the Jedi Temple. The Archives were where the Jedi kept the Holocrons, devices which contained all of their secrets.

As Anakin and Ahsoka entered the Jedi Archives, the chief librarian approached them from across the room.

Anakin acknowledged her arrival with a small

bow. "Madame Jocasta Nu," he said. "This is Ahsoka Tano. She is to be your new security officer."

Madame Jocasta looked Ahsoka over. "So good to meet you," she said. "You hardly seem old enough to be a Padawan."

"Let me show you around," Madame Jocasta said as she led Ahsoka out of the room, leaving

Anakin behind. "There is more knowledge here than anywhere else in the galaxy," she added.

Ahsoka looked around at the Jedi studying at consoles throughout the hall. "Master Kenobi says that there are even texts here that are forbidden to read."

"It is true," Madame Jocasta laughed. "The Archives hold a great many secrets."

They stopped in front of a door at the far end of the Archives.

"Beyond this door lies the Holocron vault." Madam Jocasta spoke in a serious tone. "The Holocrons contain the most closely guarded secrets of the Jedi Order."

Jedi Master Kit Fisto approached the vault.

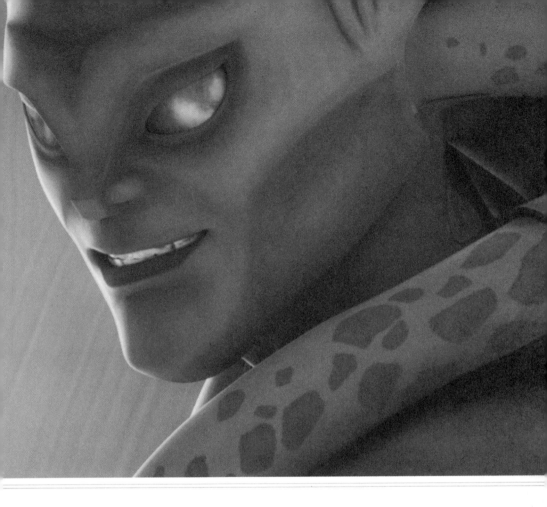

He held a Holocron in one hand and placed his
other hand on a scanner near the door. The vault
door opened and Kit vanished inside. Ahsoka
caught a glimpse of the vault before the door
closed. Safes lined the walls and each was
encased inside an energy shield. They were very
well protected.

"Can we go inside?" Ahsoka asked.

"I'm afraid not, my dear," Madame Jocasta replied. "I haven't been inside myself for years. Only members of the Jedi Council are allowed access."

Ahsoka looked longingly at the locked door.

"Guarding the Holocrons is one of the most important duties a Jedi can be given," Madame Jocasta added. "Do you think that you are up to the task?"

Ahsoka perked up a bit. "Definitely!" she replied.

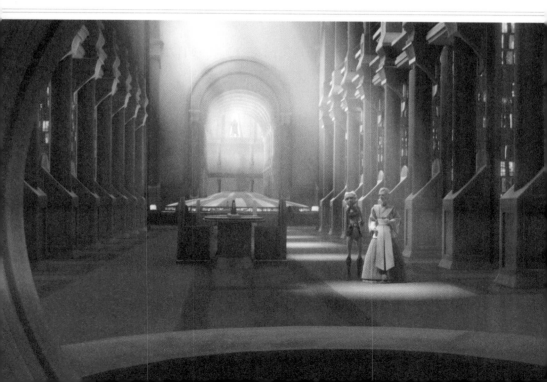

CHAPTER 2

Slivers of light came through the blinds of a dingy room in the backstreets of Coruscant. Bounty hunter Cad Bane received a hologram transmission from the Sith Lord Darth Sidious.

"I have need of your services," the Sith Lord began.

Cad Bane nodded his head. "I'm listening."

"I need a Jedi Holocron," Sidious continued.

"To get a Holocron, I'd have to break into the

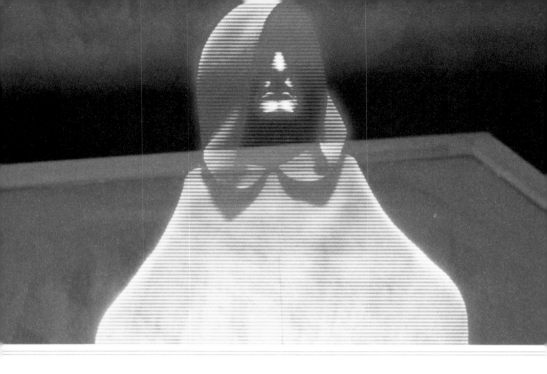

Jedi Temple," Bane laughed. "It's impossible . . . not to mention deadly."

Sidious gave the bounty hunter a hard look. "Perhaps your reputation has been exaggerated . . ."

Bane thought for a moment. "I want a rogue class starfighter with elite weapons, cloaking device, the works," he said. "Oh, and triple my usual rate."

"Yes, yes . . ." the Sith Lord agreed. "Your price is of no concern. I will also provide you the means to get inside the Temple."

"Okay," Bane replied. "You've got a deal."

Bane hunched over Todo 360, a two-foot tall service droid. Todo's back panel was open and Bane was working on it.

"You know," the droid said. "If you just tell me what it is you are doing back there, I could probably be of some assistance."

"I am just doing some maintenance," Bane said as he placed a small rectangular device with a screen into Todo. "You've been having memory crashes."

"That is preposterous, I have no memory of any crashes," the droid replied. Then it panicked.

"No memory of any crashes . . . Oh, no. I am doomed! Bane, you have to help me!"

Bane closed Todo's back panel and stood up. "Calm down," he said. "I'm done."

Just as Todo was thanking Bane, a buzzer sounded.

"Get the door," the bounty hunter ordered.

Cato Parasitti, a shape-shifting Clawdite bounty hunter, stood at the door.

The female shape-shifter walked over to Bane who was seated at a desk, looking at an image on his display screen.

"What's the mission?" Cato asked.

"We're stealing a Holocron," Bane said with a smile.

Cato looked at the bounty hunter in shock.

Bane pointed to a holographic map of the Jedi Temple.

"Our client has set us up with some help," Bane said. "For one, the map of the Temple you're looking at right now. For another, a security chip that I've placed in my droid.

Todo looked over. "I've been given all the technical data regarding the security systems in

the Jedi Temple," it said.

"Both the ventilation shafts and the vault itself are equipped with all kinds of traps and security measures," Bane continued. "Todo can take them out. But then we'll need help from someone inside the Jedi Archive Library. And that's where your talents as a changeling will come in."

Bane then gestured to a body slumped over in the corner of the room. It was the remains of Jedi Master Ord Enisence.

Cato smirked as she morphed into a likeness of the dead Jedi.

CHAPTER 3

Ahsoka stood guard at the Jedi Archive. Noticing a familiar face, she made her way over.

"Good afternoon, Master Enisence," she said, not knowing that it was the shape-shifter, Cato. "May I be of assistance?"

"No, no, thank you, my dear," Cato replied as she tried to make her way past Ahsoka. "I don't want to bother you."

The Padawan moved in front of Cato, bringing

her to a stop.

"Oh, it wouldn't be a bother at all," Ahsoka said. "Things are slow right now and I could use something to do."

"Uh . . ." Cato said nervously. "Thank you, but I'll be fine on my own."

"Are you sure?" Ahsoka asked.

Cato couldn't take it anymore. She spun around angrily and stepped toward Ahsoka.

"Look, youngling," the shape-shifter yelled. "I said that I was fine. Now let me go about my business!"

Madame Jocasta turned when she heard the outburst. Her eyes narrowed as she watched Cato suspiciously.

Ahsoka backed off as Cato took a seat at one of the many computer terminals in the room. Once she was gone, Cato pulled up a screen that displayed the Temple's security systems.

"I'm in," Cato said into her hidden comlink.

"It's about time," Bane replied. "Just tell us where to get in."

"All right," Cato continued. "There's a weak point in the shield that Todo should be able to break through. I'm beaming the coordinates now."

On the roof of the Jedi Temple, Todo hummed and whirred, then finally beeped once.

"Okay," the droid said. "I've got it."

Bane rocketed into the air with his jet pack and Todo hovered behind him. They made their way to a small opening in the energy shield that protected the Temple. They dropped down through the opening and the shield closed behind them.

"We're in," Bane said into his comlink.

CHAPTER 4

In the Jedi Temple War Room, Anakin, Obi-Wan Kenobi, and Yoda stood around a large holographic star map. Suddenly, Yoda bent over as if he were in pain.

"Master Yoda," Anakin called out. "What is it?"

Yoda waved him off and leaned against his small, wooden cane. He closed his eyes and turned his mind toward the Force. Obi-Wan and

Anakin stood silently.

"A disturbance in the Force . . ." Yoda finally spoke. "Intruders . . . in this Temple."

Anakin and Obi-Wan turned and quickly made their way through the hallways of the Temple.

"Where do we start looking for these intruders?" Anakin asked. "What could they be after?"

"Perhaps they've come to hijack starfighters," Obi-Wan replied.

"Maybe they're assassins," Anakin offered.

"No, I doubt that," Obi-Wan responded.

"They have to be after something," Anakin said. "What can they get here that they can't get anywhere else?"

The two Jedi thought for a moment and then Obi-Wan looked at his former student.

"Information," he said. "Every bit of troop information in one place."

"It's all in the east tower," Anakin said. "I'll head there right away."

Obi-Wan nodded his head in agreement. "And

I'll monitor the perimeter defenses from the central security station."

Obi-Wan stood in the central security station where he was able to monitor the whole Temple. A full-sized hologram of Anakin appeared next to him.

"I'm in the tower," Anakin said. "There are no intruders."

"But if they aren't in the tower," Obi-Wan wondered, "what are they after?"

Just then Yoda entered the room.

"The communication center, perhaps," he said, "is their target."

"They must be in the central ventilation system," Anakin added.

Obi-Wan turned to the hologram. "The vent shafts are filled with security devices," he said. "There's no way they'd get through."

"It's got to be the vents," Anakin replied. "It's the only way."

"Hold on," Obi-Wan said. "Let me check the system."

Obi-Wan flicked on the security display for the ventilation system. Red warning lights blinked wildly on the screen.

"You're right," he said. "There has been a disturbance."

Concern filled Yoda's face.

"On high alert," he said, "place the Temple."

CHAPTER 5

On the roof of the Jedi Temple, a vent grating had been pushed aside. Down below, Cad Bane hung from a cord. Todo hovered just above him. Using the information that Sidious gave them on the security systems, Todo deactivated all the laser sensors in the shaft.

Below them a huge, spinning fan blocked their way.

"The control board for the fan should be on

your left," Cato instructed from over the comlink.

Todo turned to its left and hovered over to a small control panel on the side of the vent shaft.

"All clear, sir," the droid said after it had deactivated the fan.

Bane lowered himself farther down into the shaft and slipped between the blades.

Cato's voice came again from the comlink. "The fan that you're passing through has a security switch on it."

"I don't see anything," Todo replied. "Besides, we've already made it past."

As Todo was talking, it accidentally passed through a laser beam trigger that reactivated the

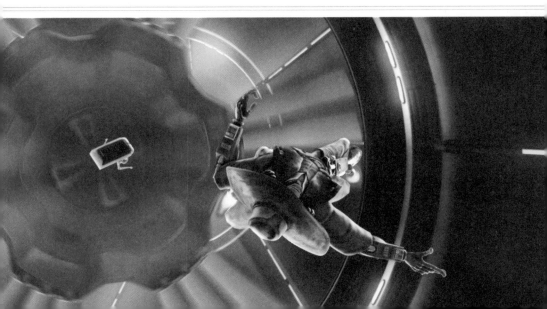

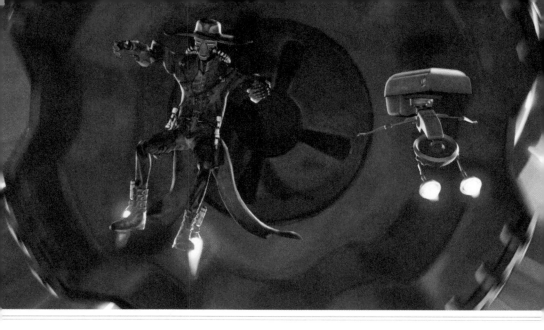

fan. The blades instantly snapped Bane's cable and he dropped straight down the ventilation shaft.

"Cato, do something!" Bane cried into the comlink.

A moment later, the fan stopped. Bane and Todo both crashed down onto the shaft floor.

Madame Jocasta sat at the main desk in the Jedi Archives. She was working away on her console when the screen suddenly began flashing red.

"Warning," a computerized voice came
from the console. "The Temple is on high alert.
Exercise caution."

"Ahsoka," Madame Jocasta called out as she
quickly stood up. "The Temple has been placed
on high alert. Watch over the central archives for
me. I must warn everyone."

"Yes, ma'am," Ahsoka replied as she
continued to stand guard. She hated the idea of
standing around while something more exciting
was happening, but she knew how important it

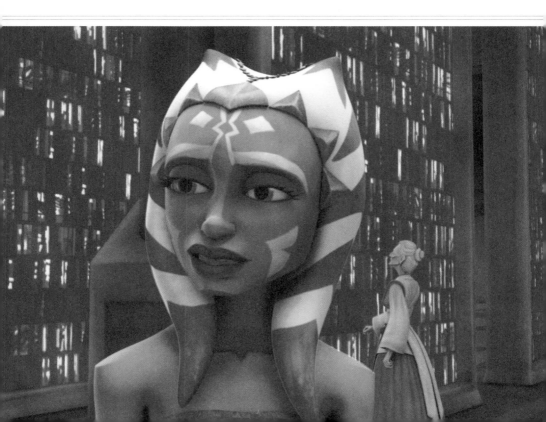

was to protect the Holocrons.

Madame Jocasta made her way over to Cato who was seated at a console. The changeling still had the appearance of Jedi Master Enisence.

"Excuse me," she said to Cato, who was whispering something into her comlink. "I don't mean to disturb you, but ..."

Just then Cato leaped up from her seat and stood face-to-face with Madame Jocasta, who looked at her suspiciously.

"The whole temple is on high alert," Madame Jocasta continued.

"Thank you," Cato said as she swung her arm and hit Madame Jocasta in the face, knocking her unconscious.

Cato looked around to make sure that no one saw what had happened, then she dragged Madame Jocasta to a corner of the room. The changeling then morphed her form into Jocasta's.

In the ventilation duct, Bane and Todo made
their way through the Temple. They stopped in
front of a large grating and looked through.

"This is it," Bane said.

"Cato, come in," Bane said into his comlink.
"We're over the vault."

"Give me a moment to check out the security
system," Cato replied.

A loud clank came from farther down in the
ventilation duct.

"Hurry it up, Cato," Bane called into the
comlink. "We can't stay hidden for long."

CHAPTER 6

Obi-Wan and Anakin stood on the roof of the Temple and looked down into the open ventilation shaft. The remains of Bane's grappling hook hung from the edge.

"Well, it looks like this is where they broke in," Anakin said.

"Fortunately, we'll have a less troublesome time," Obi-Wan added as he punched a code into a nearby control panel.

Just then a panel opened, revealing a ladder leading down the vent. The two Jedi quickly climbed down to the floor of the ventilation duct.

"Which way do you think they went?" Anakin asked as he noticed passages heading off in all directions.

"The communication center is this way," Obi-Wan said as he pointed down one of the passageways. "We'd better hurry if we're going to catch them."

Anakin and Obi-Wan made their way toward

the communication center. After a short while, Anakin stopped and shook his head.

"I don't think that they came this way," he said.

Obi-Wan agreed. "Master Yoda," he said into his comlink. "Are you picking up any other life signs in the quadrant?"

In the Temple's War Room, Yoda scanned a bank of monitors for life signs.

"Deep in the Temple," Yoda responded, "the

intruders are."

"How are they managing to stay out of our way?" Obi-Wan asked over the comlink.

"Hmmmm." Yoda thought for a moment. "Possible it is, receiving assistance they are . . . from inside."

Cato, disguised as Madame Jocasta, sat at a console in the Archives. A map of the vault was open on the screen in front of her.

"The vault is filled with laser sensors that go in every direction," she said into her comlink. "I'll try to deactivate the whole system from here."

"Just hurry," Bane called back. "The Jedi are getting closer. I can hear them."

"Okay," Cato said as she entered something into the Temple's computer. "I've got it. Go in."

As Bane and Todo looked down through the grating into the vault, they heard the sound of the laser beams powering down.

The vent grating swung down and out, and Todo floated down into the vault while Bane climbed down into the room.

Bane quickly got to work on a control panel that was next to one of the shielded safes in the vault.

"Almost there," Bane called to Todo. "Are you done deactivating those laser beams yet?"

Todo looked up from the laser emitter that it was working on.

"We are good to go," the droid said.

"Good," Bane added as he gestured toward the farthest wall from the vault door. "Start cutting through that wall."

"Cut through the wall? Why?" Todo asked.

Cato's voice came in over the comlink. "Yeah, Bane, I don't understand. The only thing on the other side of that wall is an access tunnel to the communications center."

"I know," Bane smiled.

CHAPTER 7

Ahsoka received a message from Master Yoda on her comlink.

"Padawan, alert you must be," the Jedi Master said. "Sense deception, I do. Posing as a Jedi, an intruder is."

"I've got a bad feeling about this," Ahsoka said as she looked around the room.

"Warn Master Jocasta you must," Yoda ordered the young Padawan.

Ahsoka quickly rushed off to find Madame
Jocasta.

In a far corner of the Archives, Ahsoka saw
Madame Jocasta working at a console. She could
see the Jedi Master speaking into a comlink.

As Ahsoka walked up behind her, she could
hear what was being said.

"Bane," Ahsoka heard Madame Jocasta
say. "The two Jedi have turned around and are
making their way toward you."

Ahsoka couldn't believe it. This wasn't

Madame Jocasta—it was the intruder!

"Who are you?" Ahsoka called out as she stepped up behind Cato. "What have you done with Madame Jocasta?"

Cato stayed in her seat with her back toward Ahsoka.

"The same thing that I'm going to do to you," Cato replied in a threatening voice as she drew her lightsaber and leaped from her chair.

The blade came down quick, but Ahsoka was quicker and drew her own lightsaber in time to block the attack.

In the middle of the Archives, a fierce lightsaber battle raged. Cato, still disguised as

Madame Jocasta, was doing her best to fight Ahsoka, but the Padawan was able to overtake the changeling and knock her back into the main desk of the Archive.

Cato fell to the ground and Ahsoka pointed the tip of her lightsaber to her throat.

"You may have Madame Jocasta's shape," Ahsoka said with authority, "but not her skills."

In the vault, Bane continued with his attempts to break into the safe that held the Holocrons.

"Todo," Bane called out with a frustrated grunt. "Are you done yet?"

"I'll be done when I'm finished," Todo said as

it continued to cut a hole in the wall. "These things take time."

"I'm not going to be able to do this without a diagram," Bane said as he activated his comlink. "Cato, come in. Cato?"

There was no reply from the other end, just static.

"What has happened?" Todo asked.

"Something's gone wrong," Bane said. "Todo, is that hole finished?"

"Yes, but . . ." Todo tried to say, but Bane cut it off.

"Good," he said. "Get to the communications center."

CHAPTER 8

Just as Obi-Wan and Anakin entered the vault system, Obi-Wan's comlink activated. It was Ahsoka.

"Master Skywalker," she said. "I've captured an imposter. She said that the intruders are in the Holocron vault."

Anakin turned to Obi-Wan. "They must be trying to gain access to the communication center from the vault," he said.

"Let's get in there," Obi-Wan ordered as they

took off toward the Holocron vault.

As soon as they entered the room, there was a violent explosion and the two Jedi were thrown back. As the smoke cleared, they saw the hole that Todo cut heading to the communication center.

"Quick," Obi-Wan called out as he and Anakin ran through the hole.

Once the Jedi were gone, Bane slipped out from a hiding place in a dark ventilation duct. He opened the safe door and took the Holocron.

In the Jedi Archives, a cloaked Cad Bane walked past all the Jedi, who were distracted by the explosion, and out of the Archives. On the other side of the room, he could see that Cato had been captured by the Jedi. He put his head down and kept walking.

Todo popped out of the access hatch and into the communications center. There was a group of Jedi waiting, including Yoda and Mace Windu.

Todo turned to flee, but Anakin and Obi-Wan came through the hatch and blocked the exit.

Just then a beeping sound came from Todo's backside. The droid hit his back panel and it

opened up, revealing the device that Bane had installed earlier.

"It's a bomb!" Mace Windu called out. He used the Force to hurl Todo across the room.

"Oh, no, no, no . . ." Todo cried out, but it was too late. The bomb exploded.

The Jedi were all safe, but Todo was no more.

Yoda, Obi-Wan, Anakin, and Ahsoka stood in the vault room. They had the captured Cato with them.

Yoda examined the open safe.

"Hmmm, our war operations it was never about," he said.

"If this Cad Bane is still here on Coruscant," Obi-Wan said, "I will find him."

The Jedi knew that Bane had escaped the Temple with the Holocron. He had beaten them this time. However, they would not give up. They would find Bane and get the Holocron back.